Saffron the Yellow Fairy

Daisy Meadows

Illustrated by Georgie Ripper

The Fairyland Palace

Maze

Forest

Orchard

Black Pot

Meadow

Tower

Beach

Rockpools

Rainspell Island

Jack Frost's
Ice Castle

Tom Goodfellow's
House

Merry-go-round

Mrs Merry's
Cottage

Willow
Tree

Stream

Field

Town

aid
ge

Harbour

Dolphin Cottage

Cold winds blow and thick ice form,
I conjure up this fairy storm.
To seven corners of the mortal world
the Rainbow Fairies will be hurled!

I curse every part of Fairyland,
with a frosty wave of my icy hand.
For now and always, from this
fateful day,
Fairyland will be cold and grey!

Ruby and Amber have been rescued.
Now it's time to search for

Saffron the Yellow Fairy

Contents

To the fairies at the
bottom of my garden

Special thanks to
Sue Bentley

A Very Fierce Bee

'Over here, Kirsty!' called Rachel Walker. Kirsty ran down one of the emerald green fields that covered this part of Rainspell Island. Buttercups and daisies dotted the grass.

'Don't go too far!' Kirsty's mum called. She and Kirsty's dad were climbing over a stile at the top of the field.

Kirsty caught up with her friend. 'What have you found, Rachel? Is it another Rainbow Fairy?' she asked hopefully.

'I don't know.' Rachel was standing on the bank of a rippling stream. 'I thought I heard something.'

Kirsty's face lit up. 'Maybe there's a fairy in the stream?'

Rachel nodded. She knelt down on the soft grass and put her ear close to the water.

Kirsty crouched down too, and listened really hard.

The sun glittered on the water as it splashed over big, shiny pebbles. Tiny rainbows flashed and sparkled – red, orange, yellow, green, blue, indigo, and violet.

And then they heard a tiny
bubbling voice. 'Follow me...'
it gurgled. 'Follow me...'

'Oh!' Rachel gasped. 'Did you hear
that?'

'Yes,' said Kirsty, her eyes wide.
'It must be a *magic* stream!'

Rachel felt her heart beat fast.
'Maybe the stream will lead us to
the Yellow Fairy,' she said.

Rachel and Kirsty had a special secret. They had promised the King and Queen of Fairyland they would find the lost Rainbow Fairies. Jack Frost's spell had hidden the Rainbow Fairies on Rainspell Island. Fairyland would be cold and grey until all seven fairies had been found and returned to their home.

Silver fish darted in and out of the bright green weed at the bottom of the stream. 'Follow us, follow us...' they whispered in tinkling voices.

Rachel and Kirsty smiled at each other. Titania, the Fairy Queen, had said that the magic would find them!

Kirsty's parents had stopped to admire the stream too. 'Which way now?' asked Mr Tate. 'You two seem to know where you're going.'

'Let's go this way,' Kirsty said, pointing along the bank.

A brilliant blue kingfisher flew up from its perch on a twig. Butterflies as bright as jewels fluttered amongst the reeds.

'Everything on Rainspell Island is so beautiful,' said Kirsty's mum.

5

'I'm glad we still have five days of holiday left!'

Yes, Rachel thought, *and five Rainbow Fairies still to find: Saffron, Fern, Sky, Inky – and Heather!*

Ruby the Red Fairy and Amber the Orange Fairy were already safe in the pot-at-the-end-of-the-rainbow.

The girls ran on ahead of Mr and Mrs Tate. As they followed the bubbling stream, the sun went behind a big, dark cloud.

A chilly breeze ruffled Kirsty's hair.
She saw that some of the leaves on
the trees were turning brown, even
though it wasn't
autumn. 'It looks
like Jack Frost's
goblins are still
around,' she
warned Rachel.
'I know.' Rachel
gave a shiver.
'Horrible things!
They'll do anything
to stop the Rainbow
Fairies getting
back to Fairyland.'
The two friends stared
anxiously up at the sky.
But then the sun came out
again. They smiled with relief.

The stream ran through a meadow covered with green clover. A herd of black and white cows were grazing at the water's edge. They looked up with their huge, brown eyes.

'Aren't they lovely?' Kirsty said.
Suddenly the cows tossed their heads and ran off towards the other end of the field.
Rachel and Kirsty looked at each other in surprise. What was going on?
There was a loud buzzing noise.

A small angry shape came whizzing through the air, straight towards them! Rachel almost jumped out of her skin. 'It's a bee!' she gasped. 'Run!' Kirsty cried. The cows had got the right idea!
Rachel tore through the meadow with Kirsty beside her, their feet pounding the grass. 'Keep running, girls,' called Mr Tate, catching up with them. 'That bee seems to be following us!'
Rachel glanced back. The bee was huge, bigger than any bee she'd ever seen.

'In here, quick!' Mrs Tate called from the side of the field. She pulled open a wooden gate.

They all ran through it, then stopped to get their breath.

'I wonder who lives here?' Kirsty panted. They were in a beautiful garden. A path led up to a thatched cottage with yellow roses around the door.

Just then, a very strange creature
came out from behind some trees.
It looked like an alien from
outer space!

'Oh!' Rachel and Kirsty gasped.

The creature
lifted its gloved
hands and
removed its
white helmet
to reveal...an
old lady! She
smiled at them.
'Sorry if
I startled you,' she said.
'I do look a bit strange in
my beekeeper's suit.'

Rachel sighed in relief. It wasn't
a space alien after all!

'I'm Mrs Merry,' the old lady
went on.

'Hello,' Rachel said. 'I'm Rachel. This is my friend, Kirsty.'

'And this is my mum and dad,' Kirsty added.

Mr and Mrs Tate greeted Mrs Merry.

Then Mr Tate ducked as the huge bee zoomed past his ear. 'Watch out!' he said.

'Oh, it's that hiveless queen again,' said Mrs Merry. She flapped her hand at the bee. 'Go on, shoo!' Rachel watched it swoop over a low hedge and disappear.

'Why did the bee chase us?'
Kirsty asked.

'I don't think she was chasing you,
my dear,' said Mrs Merry. 'She was
just heading this way because she's
looking for a hive of her own. But
all of mine already have queens.'

'Well, thank goodness she's gone
now!' said Mrs Tate.

'Since you're here, would you
like to try some of my honey?'
Mrs Merry asked. Her blue eyes
sparkled merrily.

'Oh, yes please,' said Rachel.

The others nodded,
and they followed
Mrs Merry across
the lawn to
a table covered
with rows
of jars.

Each jar was filled with rich golden honey. Dappled sunlight danced over the jars, making the honey glow.

'Here you are,' said Mrs Merry, spooning some honey on to a pretty, yellow plate.

'Thank you,' Rachel said politely. She dipped her finger into the little pool of honey and popped it into her mouth. The honey was the most delicious she had ever tasted – sweet and smooth.

Then she felt it begin to tingle on her tongue. She looked across at Kirsty. 'It tastes all fizzy!' she whispered.

Kirsty dipped her finger into the honey too. 'And look!' she said.

Rachel saw that the honey was sparkling with a thousand tiny, gold lights. She grabbed Kirsty's arm. 'Do you think this means—'

'Yes,' said Kirsty. Her eyes were shining. 'Another Rainbow Fairy must be nearby!'

The Magic Hive

'We have to find out where this honey came from!' Rachel said excitedly.

'Yes,' Kirsty agreed. 'Mum? Can we stay here a bit longer, please?'

'As long as it's OK with Mrs Merry,' Kirsty's mum replied.

Mrs Merry beamed. 'Of course they can stay,' she said kindly.

Mr and Mrs Tate decided to carry on with their walk. 'Make sure you come back to Dolphin Cottage by lunchtime,' Kirsty's mum said.

'We will,' Kirsty promised.

'Come along then, girls.' Mrs Merry set off across the smooth, green lawn.

Rachel and Kirsty followed her down the garden to some old and twisted apple trees. Six wooden hives stood underneath.

Kirsty stared at the row of hives. 'Which one did the honey we tasted come from?' she asked.

Mrs Merry looked pleased. 'Did you enjoy it? The honey from that hive tastes especially good at the moment.'

Rachel and Kirsty grinned at each other.

'I think we might know why,' Rachel whispered to Kirsty.

'Yes,' Kirsty agreed. 'It could be fairy honey!'

'That's the one,' Mrs Merry said proudly, pointing to the very bottom of the garden. One hive stood there all alone, beneath the biggest apple tree.

As they drew nearer to the hive, a sleepy buzzing sound drifted up into the air. 'The bees in this hive are very peaceful nowadays,' said Mrs Merry. 'I've never known them to be so happy.'

'Can we get a bit closer?' Rachel asked eagerly. She couldn't wait to find out if the hive held a magical secret!

Mrs Merry looked thoughtful. 'I think it's safe, with the bees so quiet,' she decided. 'But you had better wear a hood like mine, just in case.'

She went into a nearby shed and brought out two beekeepers' hoods. 'Here you are.'

Rachel and Kirsty pulled the hoods over their heads. It was a bit dark and stuffy inside but they could see out of the fine netting.

They moved closer to the hive. The soft buzzing sounded almost like music.

'We need to open it and have a look,' Kirsty whispered to Rachel.

Rachel nodded.

But they couldn't start searching
for the Yellow Fairy with Mrs Merry
there. Ruby had warned them
that no grown-ups should see
the fairies.

Suddenly Kirsty had an idea.
'Mrs Merry, could I have a drink
of water, please?' she asked.

'Of course you can, dear,'
Mrs Merry said. She went off
towards the cottage.

The girls waited until Mrs Merry
disappeared inside.

'Quick!' Kirsty spun round.
'Let's open the hive.'

Rachel grasped one end of the lid.
Kirsty took hold of the other end.
They pulled hard and it slowly
came loose with a squeaky sound.
Strings of golden honey stretched
down from the lid.

'Watch out. It's very sticky,'
Rachel said.

The girls bent down and laid the
heavy wooden top carefully on the
ground. Kirsty wiped her fingers on
the grass.

'Look!' Rachel whispered as she
stood up.

Kirsty turned to see, and gasped.
A shower of sparkling gold dust
shot up out of the hive. It hung in
a soft cloud, shimmering and
dancing in the sunlight. Fairy dust!

Rachel leaned over and peered
down into the hive. A tiny girl was
sitting cross-legged on a piece of
honeycomb, in the middle of
a golden sea of honey.

A bee lay with its head in her lap
while she combed its silky hair.
Several other bees were waiting their
turn, buzzing gently.

'Oh, Kirsty,' Rachel whispered.
'We've found another Rainbow
Fairy!'

Bee Friends

Rachel and Kirsty took off their hoods and stared down into the hive in delight.

The fairy had bright yellow hair. She wore a necklace of golden raindrops around her neck and sparkly golden bracelets on both wrists. Her bright yellow T-shirt and shorts were the colour of buttercups. Her delicate wings

glistened with a thousand
shimmering rainbows.

'Oh, thank you for finding
me!' the fairy said in
a tinkling voice. 'I'm Saffron
the Yellow Fairy.'

'I'm Rachel,'
said Rachel.
'And I'm Kirsty,'
said Kirsty.
'We've met two
of your sisters
already – Ruby
and Amber.'
Saffron beamed
happily.
'You've found
Ruby and Amber?'
She stood up, gently
pushing the bee away.

'Yes. They're safe in the pot-at-the-end-of-the-rainbow,' Rachel said.

Saffron clapped her tiny hands. 'I can't *wait* to see them again.' Suddenly she looked worried. 'Have you seen any of Jack Frost's goblins near here?' she asked.

'No, not here,' Kirsty said. 'But there were some by the pot yesterday.'

'We hid in a bush until they went away,' Rachel explained.

'Goblins are scary,' Saffron said in a trembling voice. 'I've been safe from them here in the hive, with my friends the bees.' Rachel felt very sorry for Saffron. 'It's all right. King Oberon sent one of his frog footmen to look after you and your sisters.' Saffron cheered up. 'I've been really worried about finding my sisters. Jack Frost's magic is so cold and strong.'

'It won't be long now,' Kirsty said. 'We are going to find Fern, Sky, Inky, and Heather too, aren't we, Rachel?'

'Yes. We promised,' Rachel agreed.

'Oh, thank you!' Saffron said. She threw out her arms and gave a shake of her sparkling wings.

Fairy dust rose into the air and drifted down around Rachel and Kirsty. Where it landed, bright yellow butterflies appeared, with tiny fluttering wings.

A large bee crawled from one of the waxy openings in the honeycomb next to Saffron.

'This is my best friend, Queenie,' said Saffron. She put her arms round the bee's neck and kissed the top of her furry head.

Queenie buzzed softly.
'She says hello,' said Saffron.
'Hello, Queenie,' Kirsty and Rachel said together.
Saffron picked up her tiny comb and began to comb Queenie's shiny hair. Another bee buzzed crossly.
'Don't worry, Petal, I'll comb your hair next,' Saffron said.

Rachel and Kirsty looked at each other in dismay.

'What if Saffron wants to stay with Queenie and the other bees?' Kirsty whispered.

'Saffron, you have to come with us!' Rachel burst out. 'Or Fairyland will never get its colours back! It will take all of the Rainbow sisters to undo his spell.'

Forgetful Fairy

'Yes, of course! We have to break Jack Frost's spell!' Saffron cried. She jumped to her feet and picked up her wand.

Suddenly an icy wind sprung up. Something crunched under Kirsty's feet. The grass was covered with frost!

Rachel shivered as something soft and cold brushed against her cheek.

A snowflake in summer? 'What's happening?' she cried.

'Jack Frost's goblins must be near,' Kirsty said, worriedly.

Saffron's tiny teeth chattered with cold. 'Oh, no! If they find me, they will stop me getting back to Fairyland!'

Kirsty looked at Rachel in alarm.

'Quick, we must go!'

Rachel leaned down
and lifted
the fairy out of
the hive.

Saffron's golden
hair dripped
with honey.

'Oh dear,
you're really
sticky,' Rachel said.

Just then Kirsty spotted
Mrs Merry coming out
of her cottage.

'I'd forgotten about asking
for a drink,' Kirsty said.
'What are we going to do?'

Rachel thought for
a moment, then popped
the fairy into the pocket
of her shorts.

Saffron gave a cry of dismay. 'Hey! It's dark in here!' she complained.

'Sorry,' Rachel whispered. 'I'll get you out again in a minute.'

Suddenly Kirsty noticed the open hive. 'We have to put the top back on!' she said.

She bent down and grasped the lid. Rachel helped lift it and they quickly put it back, just as Mrs Merry came through the trees.

'Here's your drink, dear,' said Mrs Merry, holding out a glass to Kirsty. She had taken off her strange suit, and in her other hand she was carrying a shopping basket.

'Thank you very much,' Kirsty said, taking the glass.

'Now, you girls stay as long as you like,' said Mrs Merry. 'I've just remembered I must go and buy some fish for my cat.'

Rachel watched the old lady go towards the garden gate. Then she slipped her hand into her pocket.

'You can come out now,' she said to Saffron, lifting her out.

The fairy was covered with grey fluff from Rachel's pocket. 'Achoo!' she sneezed. She brushed crossly at the bits of sticky fluff clinging to her wings. 'I'm all clogged up!' she wailed. 'I won't be able to fly.'

'We need to clean you up,' Rachel said. 'But we'll have to be quick, in case the goblins find us.'

Kirsty looked round and spotted a stone bird bath filled with clear water. 'Over there.' She pointed.

'Just what we need,' Rachel agreed. She carried Saffron over to the bird bath.

Saffron fluttered on to the edge of the bath, put down her wand, and dived in.

Splash!

The water fizzed and turned bright yellow. Lemony-smelling drops shot everywhere.

Saffron swam two circles, then she was sparkling clean. She zoomed up into the air to dry. Misty yellow trails appeared as she whooshed about. 'That's better!' she cried.

She hovered in front of Kirsty. Her wings flashed like gold in the sun. Then she swooped on to Rachel's shoulder. 'Come on, let's go to the pot-at-the-end-of-the-rainbow!'

Rachel nodded. She wanted to leave the garden before the goblins got there.

'Goodbye, Queenie!' Saffron called, waving to her friend.

Queenie looked out of the entrance to the hive. She seemed a bit sad that Saffron was going. Her feelers drooped as she waved a tiny leg and buzzed goodbye.

Saffron sat cross-legged on
Rachel's shoulder as they headed
for the woods.

Suddenly she gave a cry and flew
up into the air. 'Oh, no!' she gasped.
'I've left my wand beside the
bird bath!'

Rachel looked at Kirsty in dismay.
'We'll have to go back,' she said.

'Yes,' Kirsty agreed. 'We can't leave
a fairy wand lying about for the
goblins to find.'

'Oh, dear... Oh, dear...' Saffron zipped back and forth, wringing her hands as they went back along the path.

Rachel paused at the gate and looked into the garden. There was no sign of any goblins.

Kirsty and Rachel ran through the apple trees, straight to Queenie's hive. Saffron fluttered just above them.

Suddenly an icy blast made them all shiver. They gazed around in alarm. Icicles now hung from the apple trees, and the whole lawn was white and crunchy with frost. The goblins had arrived! And they'd brought winter to the lovely garden.

Saffron gave a cry of horror.

An ugly, hook-nosed goblin jumped up on top of Queenie's hive. His bulging eyes gleamed, and in his hand he was holding Saffron's wand!

Well Done, Queenie

'Give me back my wand!'
Saffron demanded.

'Come and get it!'
yelled the goblin rudely.
He leaped off the hive
and ran towards the
garden gate.

Kirsty gasped as another goblin
jumped down from the apple tree.

Splat! He landed on the frosty grass and set off at a run.

'Catch!' The goblin threw the wand to his friend. It flew through the air, shooting out yellow sparks.

The other goblin reached up and caught the wand. 'Hee, hee. Got it!'

'Oh, no!' Saffron gasped.

Just then, Queenie flew out of
the hive with a loud buzz. All the
other bees swarmed behind her in
a noisy cloud.

Rachel watched, her eyes very
wide. With Queenie in the lead, the
bees formed into an arrow shape
and surged after the goblins.

'Be careful, Queenie!'
pleaded Saffron.

'Get away!' The goblin shook
Saffron's wand at Queenie.

More bright yellow sparks shot out
of the wand. One of the sparks hit
Queenie's wing. Queenie wobbled in
mid-air. Then she buzzed crossly
and flew at the goblin again.

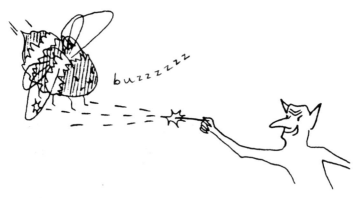

'Help!' The goblin ducked and
dropped the wand.

'Butterfingers!' grumbled the
other goblin, scooping it up.

'They're getting away!' Kirsty said in dismay.

Queenie and her bees rose into the air again.

'No, they're not!' Rachel cried excitedly. The bees shot across the garden and the goblins disappeared under an angry, black cloud.

'Get off me!' spluttered the goblin with the wand. He tried to brush the bees away, but tripped over his feet. As he fell, he bumped into the other goblin.

They tumbled over in a heap,
dropping the wand on to the grass.

'That was your fault!' complained
one of the goblins.

'No, it wasn't!' snapped the
other one.

Queenie zoomed over and
picked up the wand in her
tiny, black feet.

She carried it straight to Saffron,
who was standing on Rachel's
hand. With a little buzz, Queenie
landed next to Saffron.

Saffron took her wand from Queenie
and carefully waved it in the air.
A fountain of glittering dust and
fluttering butterflies sparkled
around them.
'My wand is all
right!' Saffron
cried joyfully.
'Look! The
goblins are
going,' Kirsty said.
The bees had chased
the goblins to the end of the
garden. Still arguing, they ran
across the fields.

As the grumbling voices faded away, the icy wind dropped. The sun shone warmly again and the frost melted. The bees streamed back and flew around Rachel and Kirsty, buzzing softly.

'Thank you, Queenie!' Saffron's eyes sparkled as she hugged her friend.

Suddenly Queenie wobbled and tipped sideways.

Rachel cupped her hands, worried that Queenie would roll off. 'I think she might be hurt,' she said. Saffron knelt down and looked closely at Queenie. 'Oh, no! She's torn her wing!' she gasped.

'It must have happened when she fought the goblin,' Rachel said.

'Can you mend Queenie's wing with magic?' Kirsty asked Saffron.

Saffron shook her head. 'Not on my own. But Amber or Ruby might be able to help me. We must take Queenie to the pot-at-the-end-of-the-rainbow at once!'

Rachel and Kirsty hurried across
the fields and into the woods.
Rachel carefully held Queenie
in her cupped hands, while
Saffron flew behind them, her
rainbow-coloured wings shimmering
in the sun.

'There's the willow tree where the
pot is hidden,' Kirsty said. She went

over and parted the branches, which
hung right down to the ground.
The black pot lay on its side in the
grass. A large, green frog hopped
out from behind it.

'Bertram!' Saffron flew down
and hugged him. 'I'm so glad
you're here!'

Bertram bowed his head. 'It's a pleasure, Miss Saffron,' he said. 'Miss Ruby and Miss Amber will be delighted to see you.'

Suddenly a shower of red and orange fairy dust shot up out of the pot, followed by Ruby and Amber.

'Saffron!' Ruby shouted. 'It really is you!'

'It's good to have you back,' Amber called happily. Kirsty and Rachel smiled as the fairies hugged and kissed each other.

The air around them fizzed with red flowers, orange bubbles and tiny, yellow butterflies.

Ruby flew on to Kirsty's shoulder. 'Thank you, Rachel and Kirsty,' she said. 'Now three of us are safe.' Then she spotted Queenie sitting on Rachel's hand. 'Who is this?' she asked.

'This is my friend, Queenie,'
Saffron explained. 'She helped me
get my wand back after the goblins
stole it.'

'Goblins?' Ruby gave a shudder.
'You were very brave to fight them.'
She flew down and
stroked
Queenie's
head.

'One of the
goblins used
my wand to
hurt Queenie's
wing. Can you help
her?' Saffron asked her sisters.

Amber thought hard. 'I could
mend Queenie's wing if I had
a fairy needle and thread,' she
said. Then she looked sad. 'But
I don't have any here on
the island.'

Then Rachel remembered something. 'Kirsty! What about the magic bags that the Fairy Queen gave us?'

'Oh, yes,' Kirsty said. She reached into her pocket and took out her bag. It was glowing with a soft, silver light. When she opened it a cloud of glitter shot up into the air. Kirsty slipped her hand into the bag. 'There's something here.' She drew out a tiny, shining needle, threaded with fine spider silk. She held it out to Amber. 'Perfect!' Amber said. She flew on to Rachel's hand.

Saffron stroked Queenie's black and yellow head. 'Don't worry,' she said. 'It's fairy magic, so it won't hurt.'

Kirsty watched as Amber carefully wove the needle in and out of the tear. The row of stitches glowed like tiny silver dots.

'Look, they're starting to fade,' Rachel said.

'Yes,' said Amber. 'When you can't see them any more, the wing is mended.'

Queenie buzzed softly. She lifted
her head and flapped her wings.
Then she zoomed into the air. Her
wing was as good as new!
She swooped down and
landed next to Amber.
Bowing her head,
she rubbed her
feelers against the
fairy's hand.
'You have
been such a good
friend to Saffron,
you must stay
with us,' said
Amber, hugging
the bee.
'Yes!' Ruby agreed. 'Please
come and live with us in the pot.'

Queenie flew over to Saffron and buzzed in her ear.

'She says she would love to,' said Saffron. 'There is a hiveless queen in Mrs Merry's garden who will take care of her bees. Come on, Queenie. Let's look at our new home.'

'Let's have a look too,' Kirsty said. Rachel crouched down beside her in the grass. They watched the fairy sisters and the queen bee go into the pot.

Saffron beamed when she saw all the tiny furniture. She sat down on a soft, mossy cushion. 'This is just like our home in Fairyland,' she said.

Then her face fell. 'But what about our sisters? They are still trapped on the island!'

'Don't worry,' Kirsty said. 'We'll find them soon.'

'Yes, we will,' Rachel agreed, jumping up. She looked at her watch. 'It's nearly lunchtime. We have to go. Goodbye, we'll see you again soon.'

The fairies looked up and waved. 'Goodbye! Goodbye!' Queenie waved a tiny leg and buzzed.

Bertram, the frog footman,
followed them out from under the
willow tree. 'Ruby, Amber and
Saffron will be safe here with me,'
he said. 'But you must take care
when you go looking for the others.
Watch out for goblins!'

'We will,' Rachel promised.

Kirsty looked back at the
pot-at-the-end-of-the-rainbow.
'Nothing will stop us finding
the other Rainbow Fairies!'
she said firmly.